# MYSTERIES OF
# SHERLOCK HOLMES

THE EXCHANGE

True or false?
Things are never
what they seem
to be.

# MYSTERIES OF SHERLOCK HOLMES

Based on the stories of
Sir Arthur Conan Doyle

by Judith Conaway

 HAMPTON-BROWN

Hampton-Brown
P.O. Box 223220
Carmel, California 93922
800-333-3510
www.hampton-brown.com

Printed in the United States of America

ISBN-13: 978-0-7362-3134-3
ISBN-10: 0-7362-3134-X

14 15 10 9

# Contents

# Introduction

Sherlock Holmes is the most popular **detective** in fiction. He is sometimes called The Great Detective. Holmes uses his excellent powers of deduction to **investigate** crimes. He often works with his good friend Dr. Watson. Sometimes the cases involve dangerous criminals. Holmes does not mind danger. He likes the excitement of solving challenging cases.

Arthur Conan Doyle created the Sherlock Holmes character. Doyle was born in Scotland in 1859. His mother was a talented storyteller. Doyle realized when he was a teenager that he had inherited her talent. However, he chose to be a doctor rather than a writer. He studied medicine at the University of Edinburgh. Doyle was impressed with Dr. Joseph Bell while he was at Edinburgh. Bell was an expert at observation and

**Key Concepts**

**detective** *n.* person who discovers facts, especially to solve a crime

**investigate** *v.* to observe or study closely

logic. Doyle used him as the model for Sherlock Holmes.

At first Doyle split his time between writing and being a doctor. He began to publish his short stories in magazines. He started writing his first novel in March 1886. It was called *A Study in Scarlet*. The novel introduced the characters of Sherlock Holmes and Dr. Watson to readers for the first time. It also made Doyle famous.

A detective story usually involves solving a **mysterious** crime. Most have at least three things in common. First, there is a crime that seems perfect. But things are never what they seem to be. Second, obvious **clues** point to a suspect who might not be guilty. Third, police investigate the crime. Often they cannot solve it. It is then that a private detective enters the story. His job is to uncover the truth that no one else can find. This kind of detective is not a member of the police team. He usually works alone. He helps the police by sharing his **suspicions** and what he knows. This is the kind of detective Sherlock Holmes is.

Doyle died in 1930. His work is still as popular with

**Key Concepts**

**mysterious** *adj.* having the qualities of surprise or wonder; unexplainable

**clue** *n.* detail or evidence that leads to the solution of a problem or crime

**suspicion** *n.* feeling of uncertainty or doubt

readers today as it was then. Modern authors continue to write Holmes stories using the character Doyle made famous. *Mysteries of Sherlock Holmes* includes three of Doyle's most famous mysteries. Can you follow the clues and solve the crimes before Holmes does?

## The Death of Sherlock Holmes

Doyle wrote more than just Sherlock Holmes stories. But his other writing didn't get as much attention. So Doyle decided to kill off his popular detective. "The Final Problem" was published in *Strand* magazine in 1893. In the story, Holmes falls to his death. Fans were outraged. Almost 20,000 people cancelled their subscriptions to *Strand* in protest. Because of popular demand, Doyle brought Holmes back to life in *The Hound of the Baskervilles*. This story was published in 1901. It became his most famous Sherlock Holmes story.

# The Adventure
# of the Speckled Band

It was early in April 1883. At this time I was living with Sherlock Holmes. We **had rooms** at 221B Baker Street.

One morning I woke up early. Holmes was standing by my bed. He was already dressed. I looked up at him in surprise. My clock showed that it was only seven. Holmes got up late, **as a rule**.

"Very sorry to wake you up, Watson," he said.

"What is it?" I asked. "A fire?"

"No. It is a young lady. She just came in. She says she must see me. **It looks like a case**, Watson. I thought you would want to be in on it from **the first**."

........................................................................................

**had rooms** lived
**as a rule** always
**It looks like a case** She may need our help
**the first** the beginning

I put on my clothes. In a few minutes I was ready. We went down to the sitting room.

A lady got to her feet. She was dressed in black. We saw that her face was gray. Her eyes looked **like those of a hunted animal**.

"Good morning," said Holmes. "My name is Sherlock Holmes. And this is Dr. Watson. He is my dear friend. Please tell us everything."

"My name is Helen Stoner," said the lady. "I am living with my stepfather. His name is Dr. Grimesby Roylott. He is the last living Roylott. The Roylotts have been at Stoke Moran for hundreds of years."

Holmes nodded. "I know the name," said he.

Miss Stoner went on. "At one time the Roylott family was one of the richest in England. But in the last one hundred years all has changed. **Five heads of the family in a row** were bad men. They did not take care of their lands. They wasted all the family's money. At last nothing was left. Nothing except a little land and a two-hundred-year-old house.

"My stepfather saw how things were. He knew he would have to **make his own way**. So he went to

...................................................................................

**like those of a hunted animal** scared, frightened

**Five heads of the family in a row** The last five leaders of the family

**make his own way** support himself financially

school and became a doctor. Then he went to India.

"In India, Dr. Roylott married my mother. My father had died just the year before. My twin sister, Julia, and I were only two years old when Dr. Roylott became our stepfather.

"My mother had some money—**a thousand pounds** a year. When she married Dr. Roylott, she made a new **will**. She left her money to him. The will also said that Roylott must take care of Julia and me.

"My mother died the year we came back to England. Dr. Roylott then took me and Julia to Stoke Moran. My mother's money was enough for all of us to live on. We could have had a good life.

"But after my mother died, my stepfather was a changed man. He made no friends around his old neighborhood. He would fight anyone he came across.

"Now everyone in the village is afraid of my stepfather. He is as strong as he is crazy. People stay out of his way.

"His only friends are a **band** of wanderers. He lets these people **camp** on his land. Sometimes he goes out and visits them in their tents.

......................................................................

**a thousand pounds** over a thousand dollars
**will** document saying who will get her things after she dies
**band** group
**camp** live, stay

"Then there are the wild animals. He brought them from India. There is a cheetah and a baboon. These two animals **have the run of the place**.

"From the first, my sister, Julia, and I had a very bad time. No one wanted to work at the house. We had to do all the work ourselves. Julia was only thirty when she died. But her hair was already getting white. You can see that my hair is getting white, too."

"Your sister is dead, then?" Holmes asked.

"She died two years ago. It is of her death that I wish to speak. My sister and I did not get many chances to leave Stoke Moran. But we have an aunt. My stepfather let Julia and me pay short visits to her house.

"On one of those visits, my sister met a young man. She fell in love with him. They planned to marry. My stepfather said nothing **against** her marriage. But less than two weeks later, Julia was dead."

Sherlock Holmes had been sitting back in his chair. But at these last words he sat up. His eyes opened.

"Please give us every little fact," said he.

"That will be easy," Helen Stoner said. "Every little bit of that night will be **burned into my mind** for the

...............................................................................................

**have the run of the place** are free and allowed to run all over

**against** bad about

**burned into my mind** in my memory

rest of my life. As I have said, the house is very old. We live in only one **wing** of it. All our bedrooms are on the ground floor. The first bedroom is Dr. Roylott's. The second bedroom was my sister's. The third bedroom is mine. There are no doors between the bedrooms. But they all open out onto the same long hall.

"On the night Julia died, Dr. Roylott went to his room early. But we knew he had not gone to sleep. Julia could smell his cigars.

"Julia never **could stand** that smell. So she came to my room. We sat there for some time, talking about her wedding. At eleven o'clock she got up to go. But then she stopped at the door. She looked back at me.

" 'Tell me, Helen,' she said. 'Have you ever heard someone whistling **in the dead of** night?'

" 'Never,' said I.

" 'You're sure you don't whistle in your sleep?' she asked.

" 'No, I don't,' I said. 'Why do you ask?'

" 'I ask because I keep hearing a whistle. I hear it about three o'clock every morning. I am a light sleeper. The whistle always wakes me up. I cannot tell where

..................................................................................

**wing** part, section

**could stand** liked

**in the dead of** very late at; in the middle of the

the whistle is coming from. Maybe it's coming from the next room. Maybe it's coming from outside. But I just thought I would ask if you had heard it.'

" 'No,' I said. 'I have not. Maybe it is those wanderers camping out there.'

" 'That must be it,' she said. Then she said good night. I heard her go down the hall. Then I heard her turn the key in the door."

"Hmm," said Holmes. "Did you always lock yourselves in at night?"

"Always. We were afraid of the cheetah and the baboon."

"**Quite so.** Please go on with your story."

"I could not sleep that night. You will remember that my sister and I were **twins**. They say twins can feel things that are happening to each other.

"It was a wild night. The wind was blowing hard. The rain beat against the window.

"All of a sudden I heard a scream. It was my sister's voice! I jumped up from my bed. I ran into the hall. It was then that I heard a low whistle! A few seconds later I heard a **clanging** sound.

......................................................................................

**Quite so.** I can understand why you would be scared of those animals.

**twins** born at the same time

**clanging** ringing, banging

"I ran to my sister's door. It started to open. My sister came to the door. Her face was white with fear. She could not stand up.

"I ran to her. I threw my arms around her. She fell to the floor. I bent over her. Then she spoke. I will never forget her voice. 'Oh, my God, Helen!' she said. 'It was the band! The **speckled** band!' And then, Mr. Holmes, she died!"

"**One moment**," said Holmes. "Are you sure about this whistle? And about the clanging sound? You are sure you heard them?"

"I am sure," said Helen Stoner.

"Was your sister dressed to go out?" asked Holmes.

"No. She was in her nightdress. We found a candle in her hand."

"Hmm. So she must have tried to make a light. What did the police say about the case?"

"They looked into it **with great care**," replied Helen Stoner. "They knew Dr. Roylott, you see. But they could not find out how Julia died. The windows were closed from the inside, with heavy bars. The walls were **thick**. The floor was thick, too. There was no

......................................................................................

**speckled** spotted
**One moment** Wait
**with great care** very carefully; in great detail
**thick** solid, hard

way any person could have come in the room—except through the door."

"And you are sure the door was locked?" Holmes asked again.

Miss Stoner said that she was sure.

Holmes shook his head. I could see he was not happy. "This **looks very bad**," he said. "Please go on with your story."

"Two years have gone by since Julia died," said Miss Stoner. "My life has been very sad. But about a month ago a man asked me to marry him. His name is Armitage—Percy Armitage. We are going to be married this spring.

"My stepfather has said nothing against the **match**. But two days ago he told me that I must move into my sister's room. He said he had to fix the wall in my room. So I moved next door—into the very room in which Julia died!

"Last night I lay there, thinking about Julia. And then I heard it! A long, low whistle! It was the same sound Julia had talked about—on the night she had died!

..........................................................................................

**looks very bad** is difficult to understand; is a mystery
**match** marriage

"I jumped up and lit a candle. I could see nothing in the room. But I could not go back to bed. I got dressed. I waited for **daylight**. And then I came right here, to ask your help."

Holmes said nothing for a long time. Then he spoke. "We must **act** right away," he said. "I will come to Stoke Moran this afternoon, Miss Stoner. Can I get into the house without Dr. Roylott knowing it?"

"Yes," she said. "He said he would be away all day."

"Good. You go back home, then," Holmes said. "We will come down on an early afternoon train."

Miss Stoner left the room.

"And what do you think of **it all**, Watson?" Holmes asked.

"It is a very **dark business**," I said.

"I am afraid it is. But we do have some clues. We have her words, 'the speckled band.' We know that a band of wanderers was camping on the land. They could have whistled. Then there was the clanging sound. That might have been a wanderer, too. It could have been the clanging of a window bar."

......................................................................

**daylight** the sun to come up
**act** do something; solve this mystery
**it all** everything she told us
**dark business** scary situation

"I see many things wrong with that idea," I said.

"So do I," said Holmes. "That is why we are going to Stoke Moran.

"Let's order breakfast, Watson. Then I **shall** walk downtown. I'll need some facts before we do anything else."

........................................................................................

**shall** will

### BEFORE YOU MOVE ON...

1. **Narrator** Reread pages 13–14. Who is telling the story?

2. **Inference** Reread pages 20–21. What makes it seem that Helen believes she will die the way Julia did?

**LOOK AHEAD** What is the speckled band? Read pages 23–30 to find out.

It was one o'clock when Holmes got back. He had a blue paper in his hand. It had **notes** and numbers all over it.

"I have seen the will of Dr. Roylott's wife," he said. "She left a thousand pounds, all right. But each girl was to get two hundred and fifty pounds when she got married. If the girls died before getting married, Roylott would get all the money. So you see why Dr. Roylott wanted Julia and Helen dead.

"We had better **get going**, Watson. And I would like it very much if you would bring your gun."

We went down to Waterloo Station. We caught the next train out. Then we found a horse and **cart** to take us to Stoke Moran.

Helen Stoner met us at the Stoke Moran gate. "I have been waiting for you!" she cried.

"Don't worry," said Holmes. "We will soon **get to the bottom of this**. Now, please show me the house."

Helen Stoner showed us where the bedrooms were. First Holmes walked along the outside of the house. He looked at the windows. He asked Miss Stoner to go into her own room and close the windows. Then he tried to

........................................................................

**notes**  writing

**get going**  go to Stoke Moran as soon as we can

**cart**  wagon, carriage

**get to the bottom of this**  find out what is happening

get in. He had no luck.

Next we went to the room where Julia Stoner had died. It was a small room with a low ceiling. Holmes sat down on one of the chairs. He looked **the whole room over**. He did not speak for a while.

"**Why, here is a bellpull**," he said. He pointed to a long rope on the wall. "In what part of the house does the bell ring?"

"Downstairs," Helen Stoner said. "My stepfather put it in two years ago. The bell is for calling the servants. But we never use it."

Holmes walked over to the bellpull. He gave it a strong tug. "Why, it is a dummy," he said. "It doesn't even ring. See? It just hangs from that wire up there. The wire above the air vent.

"And by the way—what is that air vent doing up there? An air hole should go to the outside. That one seems to go into the next room. Hmm. I think I shall have a look."

We went into Dr. Roylott's room. In it were only three things. A camp bed. A wooden chair. And a large **iron safe** with a lamp on it.

........................................................................................

**the whole room over** at everything in the room

**Why, here is a bellpull** Oh, here is a rope that rings a bell somewhere else in the house

**iron safe** heavy, locked box

Holmes tapped the safe. "What is in here?" he asked.

"My stepfather's papers," replied Helen Stoner.

"Are you sure there isn't a cat in that safe?" asked Holmes. "Look at this!" He picked up a small dish of milk.

"We don't keep a cat," said Miss Stoner. "Just the cheetah and the baboon."

"This milk would not go far with a cheetah," said Holmes. "And what's this?" He held up a small dog leash. The end of it had been tied in a loop.

I have never seen my friend's face so **dark**. We went outside. We walked up and down the yard several times. Then Holmes spoke to Miss Stoner.

"You must do exactly as I tell you," he said. "It could **mean your life**." She nodded.

"See that **inn** across the street?" asked Holmes. "We will go there now. We will watch the house from there. Tonight I want you to go to bed in your sister's room. Just as you did last night. Then wait until you hear Dr. Roylott go to bed. At that moment open and close the window. It will be a **signal** to Dr. Watson and me. Then go to your own room and wait.

---

**dark** serious
**mean your life** keep you alive
**inn** hotel
**signal** sign, hint

"Watson and I will be waiting for your signal. Then we will leave the inn. We are going to spend the night in Julia's room."

"I think you already know what happened, Mr. Holmes," said Helen Stoner. "Please tell me. How did my sister die?"

"We are not sure yet," said Holmes. "We must **leave you** now, Miss Stoner. We must not let the doctor see us. **Until tonight, then.**"

Holmes and I went to the inn to wait. We had a room from which we could see Stoke Moran. At about seven we saw Dr. Roylott get home. We knew it was he. We could hear him yelling at the boy who opened the gates.

At about nine o'clock the lights in the house went out. All was dark. Two hours passed. Then we saw a light **flash out** from the middle window.

"That's our signal," said Holmes. A moment later we were out on the dark road. A cold wind blew in our faces. We made our way over the old stone wall and across the yard. We got in through the window of Julia's room.

........................................................................

**leave you**  go
**Until tonight, then.**  We will see you tonight.
**flash out**  shine briefly

We had to be very quiet. The smallest sound might wake Dr. Roylott next door. We did not **dare have a light**, either. Roylott might see it through the air vent. So as soon as we were safe, we blew out the candle. I had my gun ready.

"Do not go to sleep," whispered Holmes. "You may **lose your life** if you do."

How shall I ever forget that long wait? I could not hear a sound. We were in the dark. We heard the clock **strike twelve**. Then one. Then two. Then three.

Suddenly I saw a flash of light. It had come through the air vent! Then all was quiet again.

In a moment I heard another sound. It was a soft hiss. It sounded like steam coming out of a **kettle**. Holmes jumped up. He lit a match. He began to beat at the wall with his stick.

"You see it, Watson?" he yelled. "You see it?"

But I saw nothing. At the moment Holmes lit the match, I had heard a low whistle. But I could not see what Holmes was hitting.

I lit the candle. Holmes's face was pale. I could see that he was afraid.

....................................................................................

**dare have a light**  risk lighting a candle
**lose your life**  die
**strike twelve**  ring when it was twelve o'clock
**kettle**  pot

I had no chance to ask what had happened. Suddenly the quiet of the night was **broken** by a scream. It was the most terrible sound I had ever heard. It made **my heart cold**. They say that people heard the cry all the way down in the village.

"What can it mean?" I asked.

"It means that it is all over," Holmes said. "Bring your gun. We will go into Dr. Roylott's room."

**A strange sight met our eyes.** The lamp stood on the safe. The safe was open. In the chair next to the safe lay Dr. Roylott. The dog leash we had seen earlier was on his lap. His dead eyes looked up at the ceiling. And around his head there was a yellow band. It had brown spots on it.

"The band!" said Holmes. "The speckled band!"

The band began to move. It lifted its head. It was a snake!

"It is a swamp adder. The most dangerous snake in India," said Holmes.

"Let's put it back in its cage."

Holmes picked up the dog leash. He looped it around the snake's head. He carried the snake to the safe

................................................................

**broken** interrupted

**my heart cold** me feel very scared

**A strange sight met our eyes.** We saw something very strange in the room.

and closed the door.

This story is getting too long. So I will not say too much about how we **broke the news to** poor Helen Stoner. Or about how we took her to her aunt's house. Or about how the police said that Dr. Roylott had died by accident. They said he had been playing with a dangerous pet.

Holmes **filled me in on his side of the case**. "As soon as I saw that bellpull, I knew," he said. "It was there for some reason. It did not ring the bell. So it must have something to do with that air vent. Then I remembered. Helen Stoner had said that Julia could smell cigar smoke. So that air vent must go into Dr. Roylott's room!

"Dr. Roylott had a cheetah and a baboon. Why not a snake, too? I was **doubly** sure as soon as I saw the dish of milk. Roylott had trained the snake to crawl through the vent and down the rope. The snake would come back when he whistled! The clang that Helen heard? That was the safe door closing.

"I knew the doctor would try the snake trick again. This time Helen would be killed. So I waited. When I

........................................................................................

**broke the news to**  told

**filled me in on his side of the case**  told me how he solved the case

**doubly**  even more; especially

heard the snake hiss, I hit."

"You drove the snake back into the other room," said I.

"Yes," said Holmes. "I hit the snake so hard it was **good and mad**. So it **turned on its owner**. In a way, I was the one who made Dr. Roylott die."

Holmes sighed and picked up his pipe. "I cannot say that I am very sorry," he said.

........................................................................................

**good and mad** very mad; very angry

**turned on its owner** attacked Dr. Roylott

**BEFORE YOU MOVE ON...**

1. **Summarize** The speckled band is a snake that Dr. Roylott used to kill Julia. How did he kill her? Reread pages 28–29.

2. **Character** Describe Sherlock Holmes. Why do you think Dr. Watson works with him?

# The Redheaded League

Sherlock Holmes still lives in our old rooms at 221B Baker Street. I **called upon him** there one day last fall.

I found Holmes **deep in talk**. With him was a fat old man who had bright red hair.

"Come in, Dr. Watson!" Holmes cried. "Meet Mr. J. B. Wilson. Mr. Wilson, this is Dr. Watson. He works with me on many of my cases."

The fat man got up and **made me a little bow**. Holmes sat back. He put his fingers together. (He often does that when he is thinking.) He smiled.

"Watson, my dear man, I know you love strange stories as much as I do. Mr. Wilson here has just started telling his tale. And it's one of the strangest stories I have ever heard."

........................................................................

**called upon him**  went to see him

**deep in talk**  having a serious conversation with someone

**made me a little bow**  bent at the waist in a respectful greeting

Mr. Wilson looked proud. He pulled a piece of paper out of his coat pocket. "Look at this **notice**, Dr. Watson," he said. "You may read it for yourself."

I took the paper from him.

### To All Redheaded Men

There is a job open at the Redheaded League. The pay is 4 pounds a week. The work is not very hard. To get the job you must have red hair. You must be a man over 21 years old. Come in person on Monday, at 11 o'clock, to 7 Fleet Street. Ask for Duncan Ross.

"What can it mean?" I asked.

Holmes **gave a chuckle**. "It is a little odd, isn't it? Do tell us more, Mr. Wilson."

"I own a store at Coburg Square," said Wilson. "It's a very small place. **Of late years** it has not done much more than **give me a living**. I used to have two helpers. Now I can pay only one. I can pay him only because he will work for half pay. I don't know what I

---

**notice** advertisement
**gave a chuckle** laughed
**Of late years** For the past few years
**give me a living** provide money for food and bills

would do without him."

"Hmm. A good helper who works for half pay," said Holmes. "And what is the name of this nice young man?"

"Vincent Spaulding," replied Wilson. "Oh, Vincent does have his problems. He is always down in the basement. He plays with all those cameras of his down there. **A real photo nut.** But **on the whole** he's a very good worker.

"One day about eight weeks ago, Spaulding came into my room. He had this paper in his hand. 'I tell you, Mr. Wilson,' Spaulding said, 'I wish *I* were a red-headed man. Here's another job open at the Redheaded **League**.'

"Now, I had never heard of the Redheaded League. I don't **get out** too much. But Spaulding knew all about it.

"He told me that the league had been started by Ezekiah Hopkins. Hopkins was an American millionaire. He had bright red hair.

"All his life people made fun of Hopkins because of his red hair. Then Hopkins came to London. In London

........................................................................................

**A real photo nut.** He really loves taking pictures.

**on the whole** for the most part; mostly

**League** Group, Club

**get out** leave the house or my store

he got rich. So he loved London. And he felt sorry for men with red hair. So when he died, Hopkins left his money to the red-headed men of London.

"Now, as you may have noticed, my hair is very red. So it was easy for Spaulding to **talk me into giving the job a try**. 'What have you got to lose?' he asked me.

"That was a Monday. It's always a slow day at the store. So we shut the shop. Spaulding went with me to Fleet Street.

"I never saw such a sight. Fleet Street was packed with red-headed men. The street looked like a wagon full of oranges. I saw every shade of red you can think of. Orange red. Brick red. Irish setter red.

"I was ready to give up and go home. But Spaulding would not **hear of it**. I do not know how he did it. But he pushed and pulled. At last he got me to the door.

"We joined the line going up the steps. There was another line of men coming down. They were men who had **been turned down**.

"Our line kept moving. Soon we found ourselves in a room on the second floor. There was nothing in the room except two chairs and a table. Behind the table

---

**talk me into giving the job a try** convince me to apply for the job

**hear of it** let me

**been turned down** not gotten the job

sat a small man. His hair was as red as mine. This man looked over each new **job hunter**. He found some small reason to say no to each one.

"But my turn was different. The redheaded man took one look at me. Then he got up and closed the door. He shook my hand. 'I'm Duncan Ross,' he said.

"I was too afraid to say anything. So my helper spoke for me. 'This is J. B. Wilson,' said Spaulding. 'He's here about the job with the Redheaded League.'

"'And he's **just right** for it!' cried Duncan Ross. 'I don't think I have ever seen such a **fine** head of hair.'

"Ross stepped over to the open window. 'The job has been taken!' he shouted. One by one the men below all went away. Soon Mr. Duncan Ross and I were the only redheads in sight.

"Ross turned to me. 'How soon can you start your new job?'

"'Uh, I don't know . . .' said I. 'You see, I have a small store—'

"Vincent Spaulding **broke in**. 'Oh, don't worry about the store, Mr. Wilson,' he said. 'I can take care of that for you.'

...................................................................................

**job hunter** person who wanted the job
**just right** the perfect person
**fine** nice, wonderful
**broke in** interrupted our conversation

"So I said I would work for Mr. Ross. I was to come to Fleet Street every day between ten and two. My job? Well, you are not going to believe this. All I had to do was to copy the *Encyclopedia Britannica*. That's all. And for that I would be paid four pounds a week!

"I walked out of there feeling very pleased with myself. But not for long. Quite soon I began having **second thoughts**. This all had to be some kind of joke. I just couldn't believe that story about Ezekiah Hopkins.

"But as my helper had said, I had nothing to lose. So I **showed up at** Fleet Street the next day at ten.

"To my surprise, everything went just as Mr. Ross had said it would. I went to Fleet Street every day. I copied the encyclopedia. Every Saturday Mr. Ross would come in and pay me four pounds.

"Things went on this way for eight weeks. I copied out all the facts about animals. About apples. About Africa. I began to get tired of the A's. I hoped to finish soon and get on to the B's. Then all at once **the whole business came to an end**."

"What? To an end?" asked Sherlock Holmes.

"Yes, sir," said Wilson. "It happened only this

.................................................................................

**second thoughts** doubts, concerns
**showed up at** went to
**the whole business came to an end** my job ended

36

morning. I went to work at ten o'clock. When I got there I found this card on the door."

**The Redheaded League no longer exists.**
October 9, 1890

Sherlock Holmes and I read this card. We looked at J. B. Wilson's face. The funny side of his story made us **forget ourselves**. We laughed until we roared.

"I can't see that it's very funny," cried Mr. Wilson. His face turned as red as his hair. "If you're going to make fun of me, I'll leave."

"No, no. Don't go," said Holmes. "I very much want to hear your story. I have a feeling it could be something very important."

"Why, of course it's important," said Mr. Wilson. "I have lost four pounds a week!"

"**Come, come**, Mr. Wilson," said Holmes. "You have lost nothing. You are thirty-two pounds richer than you thought you would be. **To say nothing of what you now know about things starting with A.**"

"But I want to know what it was all about!" Mr.

..........................................................................................

**forget ourselves** laugh

**Come, come** Calm down

**To say nothing of what you now know about things starting with A.** You also learned a lot.

Wilson said. "That's why I came to you, Mr. Holmes. Can you find out for me?"

"I will do my best," said Holmes. "But first—a question. This Vincent Spaulding. This helper of yours. What does he look like?"

"Well, he's small. But very quick and strong. About thirty years old. He has a **patch** of very white skin on his face."

Holmes sat up straight. He was very excited. "That's enough, Mr. Wilson," he said. "You may go home now. Today is Saturday. By Monday I will **have your answer**."

When Wilson had gone, Holmes turned to me. "Well, Watson," he asked. "What do you make of it?"

"I make nothing of it," I answered. "It is very strange. What are you going to do?"

"Go **hear some** music," replied Holmes. "There is a violin concert at St. James's Hall this afternoon. Come along. We have time to make a stop on the way."

---

**patch** small section

**have your answer** be able to tell you what happened; have solved the mystery

**hear some** listen to

**BEFORE YOU MOVE ON...**

1. **Cause and Effect** Reread pages 36–37. What happens to Wilson's Redheaded League job?

2. **Inference** Reread page 38. Why do you think Holmes asks Wilson to describe Spaulding?

**LOOK AHEAD** Read pages 39–46 to find out who Holmes suspects is tricking Wilson.

We took the underground train to Aldersgate. A short walk, and we were in Coburg Square.

One of the corner houses **wore** a sign that read "J. B. Wilson." Holmes stopped in front of the house. He thumped on the sidewalk with his stick. He pounded in two or three more spots. Then he walked up and knocked on the door.

Mr. Wilson's helper answered. He was a bright, clean looking young man.

"So sorry to bother you," said Holmes. "But can you tell me how to get to the Strand?"

"Third right, fourth left," the young man answered. He closed the door.

"That," said Holmes as we walked away, "is the fourth smartest man in London. I have come across him before. Did you **get a look at** his knees?"

"What about his knees?" I asked. "What do you know, Holmes? Why did you pound the sidewalk like that?"

"My dear doctor," said Holmes. "This is no time to talk. This is the time to look. Let's see what **lies behind this quiet block**." We turned the corner.

......................................................................

**wore** had

**get a look at** see

**lies behind this quiet block** is behind these buildings

To my surprise, we found ourselves on a busy street. "Let's see," said Holmes. "There's a cigar store. And there's the City Bank. And there is a restaurant. Hmm, yes . . ."

He turned to me. "I'll want your help," he said. "Can you be ready at ten tonight? Good. See you then. Oh, and Dr. Watson. Do you have your gun? You had better bring it along."

He waved his hand. Then he disappeared.

I got back to Baker Street just before ten o'clock that evening. Two horse-drawn **cabs** were waiting outside. Inside, I found two men with Holmes.

"Ah! We are all here now!" Holmes said. "You know Inspector Jones of **Scotland Yard**, don't you, Watson? And this is Mr. Merryweather."

Mr. Merryweather was long, thin, and sad-faced. He wore a very shiny top hat. He did not look at all happy. "This had better not be a **wild-goose chase**," he said. "I'm missing my Saturday night card game. First time in twenty years."

Holmes laughed. "You'll play a more exciting game tonight," he said. "You, Mr. Merryweather, **stand to**

.................................................................................

**cabs** carriages
**Scotland Yard** the London police force
**wild-goose chase** pointless meeting
**stand to** may; could possibly

win or lose thirty thousand pounds. And you, Mr. Jones? You stand to get your man."

"That's right!" cried Inspector Jones. "John Clay. Killer. Robber. He's a young man. But he's **at the top of the crime heap**.

"Yes—he's quite a man, John Clay. The grandson of a duke. Went to the high-class schools. **His head is as quick as his fingers.** I've been **on his trail** for years. I've never even **set eyes on** him yet."

"I hope you will meet him tonight," said Holmes. "Let's go. Two cabs are waiting outside. You two men take the first cab. Dr. Watson and I will follow in the second."

Holmes did not say much during the long drive. We drove through the dark streets. Soon we got to the busy street near Mr. Wilson's house.

Merryweather and Jones were there ahead of us. We followed Mr. Merryweather down a narrow alley. There was a side door there. He opened it. Inside was a small hall. At the end of the hall there was a heavy gate. Merryweather opened that, too. Then we went down some narrow stone stairs. There was another heavy gate

........................................................................................

**at the top of the crime heap**  committed many crimes
**His head is as quick as his fingers.**  He is very smart.
**on his trail**  trying to catch him; chasing him
**set eyes on**  seen

at the bottom.

Merryweather stopped to light a lamp. He opened the gate and we passed into a large room. It was piled with boxes.

Holmes held the lamp up to the roof. "Looks as if no one can get in from above," he said.

"Or from below," added Merryweather. He tapped the floor with his cane. "Why—dear me! It sounds **hollow**!" he cried.

"Quiet now!" whispered Holmes. "Please sit down on one of these boxes. And do try not to get in the way. Your shouting has already put us in danger."

Merryweather looked **hurt**. But he sat down.

"We have at least an hour to wait," Holmes said. "They will do nothing until our red-haired friend is in bed. After that they will not **lose a minute**.

"By now, Dr. Watson, I'm sure you know where we are," Holmes went on. "We are in a room under the City Bank. Mr. Merryweather here is the **head** of the bank. I'll let him tell you why John Clay will soon enter this basement."

"It is our French gold," the banker whispered. "Over

...................................................................................

**hollow** like there is empty space below here
**hurt** upset, offended
**lose a minute** waste any time
**head** man in charge of

thirty thousand pounds' worth." He bit his nails and looked sad. "We were afraid something like this would happen."

"Don't worry," said Holmes. "It will all be over soon. And now we must cover the lamp. I'm afraid we will have to wait in the dark. But first let's get **in place**. These are very dangerous men. We will have to be careful. I will hide behind this box. You men hide over there. Wait till I flash the light. Then **close in on** them. Watson, keep your gun ready. If they fire, shoot them down **in their tracks**."

I bent down behind a wooden box. I kept my gun hand on top of the box. I was ready for anything.

How long that wait seemed! Later I learned that we had waited only an hour and **a quarter**. But it felt like all night. I tried not to move. I was afraid to make a sound. I could hear the other men breathing.

Suddenly my eyes caught a flash of light on the floor. The flash got larger. It became a yellow line. Then a hole opened. A hand came out of the hole. It was a thin, white hand.

The hand felt the floor around the hole. Then

........................................................................................

**in place**  to our hiding places
**close in on**  grab, surround
**in their tracks**  right away; where they stand
**a quarter**  fifteen minutes

everything went dark again.

But not for long. There was a tearing sound. The hole in the floor got bigger. Over the edge peeped the face of a young man. There was a patch of bright white skin on his forehead. The young man pulled himself up into the room.

A second later he pulled a second young man up. The second man was also small and thin. He had a pale face. His hair was bright, bright red.

At that second Sherlock Holmes flashed the light.

"Great Scott!" yelled the first man. "Jump, Archie!"

"**It's no use**, John Clay," said Holmes. "You have no chance at all."

Inspector Jones had the handcuffs ready.

"Don't you touch me with your dirty hands," said John Clay. "**I have noble blood**, you know." The cuffs closed around his wrists.

"**You see it all now**, Watson," said Holmes. It was early the next morning. We were back at Baker

..................................................................................

**It's no use**  Do not even try to escape

**I have noble blood**  I come from a very important family

**You see it all now**  You now understand everything that happened

Street drinking tea. "There was only one reason for the Redheaded League. That was to get our old friend Mr. Wilson out of his store. You may think it was an **odd** way to do it. But I can hardly think of a better one.

"Of course what gave them the idea was Mr. Wilson's red hair. By chance it happened to be the same color as Archie's hair. So Archie became . . ."

"Mr. Duncan Ross!" I cried.

"Quite so. And John Clay became Vincent Spaulding. Remember how he was always in the basement? He said it was for photography. But I knew better as soon as I saw his knees. They were dirty. It **was proof** that he had been digging.

"Then I tapped the sidewalk in front of the house. No—he wasn't digging out that way. So he must be digging toward the back of the house. We walked around the block. And there I saw the City Bank."

Suddenly Holmes laughed. "Do you know what a red herring is, Dr. Watson? It's a false clue that is meant to lead us away from the real clues. Well, you've got to

......................................................................................

**odd** strange
**was proof** showed me; was evidence

**hand it to John Clay**. He's not only smart. He's funny. Don't you get it? The Redheaded League was just a red hairing, all along!"

........................................................................

**hand it to John Clay** give John Clay credit

**BEFORE YOU MOVE ON...**

1. **Foreshadowing** Holmes suspects Wilson's helper is tricking him. How can you tell? Reread pages 39–40.

2. **Plot** Reread pages 45–46. How does Holmes solve the case?

# The Adventure
# of the Blue Carbuncle

It was the second morning after Christmas. I called on my friend Sherlock Holmes to **give him good wishes for the holiday**.

I found the great detective lying on the sofa. He was smoking his favorite pipe. Next to the sofa **stood** a chair. On the chair's back there hung a black hat. The hat was dirty and torn.

A magnifying glass lay on the seat of the chair. Holmes had been looking at the hat.

"You know Peterson, the **doorman**?" asked Holmes.

"Yes," said I.

"He found this hat. He brought it here this morning—along with a good, fat goose. Right now the

........................................................

**give him good wishes for the holiday** tell him I hope he had a very nice Christmas

**stood** was

**doorman** man who opens the door; servant

goose is cooking over Peterson's fire.

"**The facts are these.** It was four o'clock on Christmas morning. Peterson was walking home late. He had been at a little party. Peterson could see a man walking ahead of him in the **gaslight**. He was a tall man. He carried a white goose over his shoulder.

"The tall man got to the corner of Goodge Street. Just then a **gang of toughs** came into the street. One of the toughs knocked off the tall man's hat. The tall man tried to fight back with his stick. Instead, he broke the window behind him.

"Peterson **rushed up** to help the tall stranger. But at the sound of the breaking glass, the man dropped the goose and ran. The gang of roughs ran away, too. So Peterson was left with the goose—and this hat."

"Which, surely, he gave back to the owner?" asked I.

"My dear fellow. There lies the problem. True, we know the *name* of the owner. See? Here's a small card that was tied to the left leg of the goose. The card says, 'For Mrs. Henry Baker.' Then, here are the letters 'H. B.' inside the hat. So we're pretty sure the tall man

...........................................................................

**The facts are these.** Here is what happened.

**gaslight** light from the streetlamps

**gang of toughs** group of criminals

**rushed up** hurried; quickly went

was Henry Baker. But there are thousands of people named Baker in London. And *hundreds* of them must be named Henry.

"Well, Peterson brought the hat to me. He kept the goose as long as he could. But today it had to be cooked or it would **spoil**. So Peterson took the goose home. He left the hat for me."

At that moment the door flew open. Peterson, the doorman, rushed into the room. His face was red.

"The goose, Mr. Holmes! The goose, sir!" he gasped.

"What about it?" asked Holmes.

"See here, sir! See what my wife found inside!" He held out his hand. There lay a shining blue stone. It was no bigger than a bean in size. But it was so pure and bright that it twinkled like a star.

Sherlock Holmes sat up with a whistle. "**By Jove**, Peterson!" said he. "This is a treasure indeed. I suppose you know what you have there?"

"Not the Countess of Morcar's **blue carbuncle**!" I broke in.

"**The very same**," Holmes replied. "I ought to know this stone's size and shape. Haven't I been reading

........................................................................

**spoil** not be safe to eat
**By Jove** It is amazing
**blue carbuncle** precious blue stone
**The very same** Yes

about it in *The Times* every single day? The countess says she will give whoever finds it a thousand pounds."

"If I remember **rightly**," I put in, "the countess lost the stone at the Hotel Cosmopolitan."

"That's right," said Holmes. "It was on December twenty-second—just five days ago. The police have arrested a plumber named John Horner. I have the story here, I think."

He found the page he was looking for. He read the news story out loud.

## Jewel Robbery at Hotel Cosmopolitan

John Horner, a plumber, was arrested today. The police say he stole a jewel from the jewel case of the Countess of Morcar. The jewel is known as the blue carbuncle.

Horner was arrested because of a story told by James Ryder. Ryder works for the hotel. Ryder said that he took Horner to the Countess of Morcar's room to fix a pipe. That was on the

........................................................................

**rightly** correctly

very day of the robbery.

Ryder stayed in the room for a while. But he **was called away**. Horner was left in the room alone.

When Ryder got back, Horner was nowhere around. But the dresser had been **forced open**. A jewel box was lying on the dressing table. The box was empty.

The police say that Horner put up a fight when he was arrested. "I didn't do it!" Horner had cried. But Horner had once **served time for robbery**. So the judge put him in jail while the Court waited for proof. When Horner heard that he was not free, he fainted.

"Hmm," said Holmes. "So much for what the police know." He threw the paper to one side. "Well, well, Watson! The question now is this: How did the stone get out of the box and into the bird?

"Here is the stone. The stone came from the goose. The goose came from Henry Baker. So now, we must **set ourselves** to find Henry Baker.

"Give me a pencil, please. And that slip of paper."

......................................................................................

**was called away** had to leave briefly
**forced open** broken into
**served time for robbery** been in prison for stealing
**set ourselves** try

Holmes wrote this note:

> Found. At the corner of Goodge
> Street, a goose and a black felt hat.
> Mr. Henry Baker can have **the same**
> by coming to 221B Baker Street at
> 6:30 this evening.

"There. **That's clear.**" Holmes handed the paper
to the doorman. "Here, Mr. Peterson. Please see that
this note is put in all the evening papers. The *Globe.*
The *Star.* The *Evening News.* The *Echo.* And any other
newspapers you can think of."

"Very well, sir," said Peterson. "And the stone?"

"Ah, yes. I will keep the stone. Thank you. And, I
say, Peterson—just buy a goose on the way back. We
must have another bird to take the place of the one your
family is now eating."

After Peterson left, Holmes picked up the stone. He
held it against the light. "It's a **bonny** thing," he said.
"Just see how it glints and sparkles. Of course it makes
**crimes happen**. Every good stone does."

....................................................................................

**the same** these items back
**That's clear.** He will come.
**bonny** beautiful
**crimes happen** people want to steal it

"Do you think this man Horner took the stone?" I asked.

"I cannot tell," replied Holmes.

"What about Henry Baker?" I went on.

"I think Henry Baker probably **had nothing to do with it**," Holmes said. "But I shall find out for sure as soon as Henry Baker **answers my ad**. Until then, I can do nothing."

"In that case," said I, "I shall keep going **on my rounds**. I have sick people to visit. I'll come back tonight, if I may. I'd like to see how this all will end."

"I'll be glad to see you," said Holmes. "Stay for dinner at seven."

..........................................................................

**had nothing to do with it** did not steal the stone
**answers my ad** reads my note and arrives here
**on my rounds** to check on my patients

**BEFORE YOU MOVE ON...**

1. **Paraphrase** On page 51, Holmes says, "So much for what the police know." What does he mean?

2. **Sequence** What events lead Holmes to the decision to look for Henry Baker?

**LOOK AHEAD** Read pages 54–61 to find out if Henry Baker is the thief.

It was six thirty before I found myself back in Baker Street. As I got near the house, I saw a tall man waiting. The tall man and I entered together.

Holmes rose from his seat. "Mr. Henry Baker, I believe," he said. "Please **take this** chair by the fire. You look cold. Ah, Watson, you have just come at the right time. Is that your hat, Mr. Baker?"

"Yes, sir. It is my hat."

"About the bird," Holmes went on. "I'm sorry, but we had to eat it."

"**To eat it!**" Mr. Baker half rose from his chair. He was very upset.

"Yes. The bird would have spoiled had we *not* eaten it. But here is another goose instead. It is about the same size as the other. Won't it **do just as well**?"

"Oh, of course, of course," said Mr. Baker.

Sherlock Holmes looked at me. I could tell Mr. Baker had **passed the test**. It was clear that he knew nothing about the jewel.

"There is your hat, then. And there is your bird," said Holmes. "By the way, could you tell me where the other goose came from? I have never tasted a better

........................................................................................

**take this** sit in this

**To eat it!** You ate the bird?!

**do just as well** be as good as the other bird

**passed the test** proved his innocence

goose."

"It came from the Alpha Inn," Baker replied. "I go there almost every night. This year the owner started a **goose club**. My friends and I gave a few pennies each week. Then at Christmas we each got a goose. The rest of the story you know. I thank you very much, Mr. Holmes, for all you have done."

Mr. Baker bowed to us and went on his way. Holmes closed the door after him. "So much for Henry Baker. Are you hungry, Watson?"

"Not very," I answered.

"Then let's save dinner until later. We can **follow up this clue while it is still hot**."

It was a bitter-cold night. We put on our overcoats and wrapped up our throats. Outside the stars were shining coldly in a cloudless sky. Our breaths looked like smoke. **Our steps rang sharply** on the pavement.

Fifteen minutes later we were at the Alpha Inn. Holmes asked for two glasses of beer. The owner brought them to us.

"Your beer should be wonderful if it is as good as your geese," said Holmes to the owner.

......................................................................

**goose club** club to save money to buy a goose

**follow up this clue while it is still hot** go find out more information right now

**Our steps rang sharply** We could hear our loud footsteps as we walked

"My geese?"

"Yes. I was talking just a while ago to Mr. Henry Baker. He was in your goose club, I think."

"Ah, yes! I see. But you see, sir, **them's not** *our* geese. I got two dozen of them from a man named Breckinridge. He sells meat over at Covent Garden."

"I thank you," said Holmes. "**Here's to your health, sir.** Good night."

We went out again into the frosty air. "Now for Mr. Breckinridge," Holmes said as he buttoned his coat.

We zigzagged through the back streets. Soon we were in the Covent Garden market. We saw the name Breckinridge on one of the largest stalls. The owner was a horsey looking man. He had a sharp face. He and a small boy were just closing up.

"Good evening. It's a cold night," said Holmes. "You **are sold out of geese**, I see."

"I can let you have five hundred geese in the morning," the man replied.

"That won't do," said Holmes. "I want the same kind of geese you sold to the Alpha Inn. They were fine birds. Where did you get them?"

................................................................................

**them's not**  those are not

**Here's to your health, sir.**  We wish you good health, sir.

**are sold out of geese**  do not have any more geese left to sell

To my surprise, the question made Breckinridge angry.

"Now then, mister," he said. "What is all this about? I haven't heard anything else all day. 'Where did you get all the geese? Who did you sell the geese to?' You would think they were the only geese in the world. People are **making such a fuss** about them."

"Well, I have nothing to do with the others who have been asking," Holmes said. He sounded as if he did not care very much about it. "You won't tell us. So we'll have to **call off the bet**. You see, I've bet five pounds those Alpha Inn geese were raised in the country."

"Then you will lose," said Breckinridge. "Those geese were raised here in town."

"You'll never make me believe that."

"Will you bet, then?" Breckinridge asked.

"That would just be stealing your money," answered Holmes. "But I'll **take you on**."

Breckinridge laughed. He called the small boy to his side. "Bring me the books, Bill," said he.

"Now, then, **Mr. Know-It-All**," he went on. "You see this little book? This is the list of folks from whom

---

**making such a fuss**  talking a lot

**call off the bet**  stop the contest

**take you on**  have a contest with you

**Mr. Know-It-All**  you think you know everything

I buy. The numbers tell where to find them in the big book. See this page? It's in black ink. Those are my country goose-raisers. See this list in red? Those are my town people. Now, look at that third name. Just read it to me."

Holmes read. "Mrs. Oakshott, 117 Brixton Road. Number 249."

"**Quite so.** Now look up that number in this big book."

Holmes turned a page. "Here you are. Mrs. Oakshott, 117 Brixton Road. Eggs and Birds."

"Now," said Breckinridge. "What is the last thing it says there? 'December twenty-second. Twenty-four geese. At seven and a half shillings. Sold to the Alpha Inn at twelve shillings.'

"Well? What do you say now?" Breckinridge asked.

Holmes **turned red**. He took a coin from his pocket. He threw it down on the table. He turned away **with an air of disgust**.

We walked a little way down the street. Then Holmes began laughing to himself. "I saw a **horse-racing form** in that man's pocket," he said.

......................................................................................

**Quite so.** Yes.
**turned red** looked embarrassed; blushed
**with an air of disgust** as if he were upset
**horse-racing form** paper with bets on horses

"You can always use a bet with a man like that. It's the sure way to get what you want. We are **near the end**, Watson. Let's go home for dinner. We can visit Mrs. Oakshott tomorrow."

Just then there were shouts behind us. We turned. There was trouble back in Mr. Breckinridge's stall! Breckinridge was yelling at a little rat-faced man. "I've had enough of you and your geese!" he shouted. "I wish you were all dead. Get away or I'll **set the dog on** you! Get out! Out!"

"Ha! This may save us that visit to Mrs. Oakshott tomorrow!" said Holmes. "Come, Watson. Let's see who this fellow is."

Holmes and I walked fast. Soon we were right behind the little man. Holmes touched the man's back. He jumped. His face turned white. "Who are you? What do you want?" he cried.

"Excuse me," said Holmes. "But I couldn't help hearing your questions about the geese. I believe I can help you."

"Who are you? And how can you know anything of this?"

........................................................................................

**near the end** getting close to solving this mystery
**set the dog on** have the dog attack

"My name is Sherlock Holmes. It is my business to know things. I know you're looking for a goose. The goose was **grown** by a Mrs. Oakshott. It was then sold to Breckinridge. He **in turn** sold the goose to the Alpha Inn. The owner of the Alpha sold the goose to a Mr. Henry Baker."

"Oh, sir, you're just the person I need!" the little man cried.

"In that case, come over to my place," said Holmes. "It's better to be warm while we talk. Before we go, will you tell me your name?"

The man looked to one side. "John Robinson," he said.

"No, no, the *real* name," Holmes said sweetly.

**Red spots came into the man's white face.** "Well, then," said he. "My real name is James Ryder."

"That's right," said Holmes. "You work at the Hotel Cosmopolitan. Step into this cab, Mr. Ryder. I shall soon be able to tell you everything you want to know."

........................................................

**grown** raised

**in turn** then

**Red spots came into the man's white face.** The man turned red from embarrassment.

**BEFORE YOU MOVE ON...**

1. **Summarize** Reread page 54. How does Holmes test Henry Baker?

2. **Cause and Effect** Reread pages 57–59. What makes Holmes think he can trick Breckinridge?

**LOOK AHEAD** Read pages 61–65 to find out if Mr. Ryder is the jewel thief.

The little man looked at Holmes. He was not sure
if this was wonderful or terrible. At last he got in. Half
an hour later we were back in Baker Street. **Not one
word had been said** during our drive.

"Here we are!" said Holmes cheerily. "That fire
looks very nice. You look cold, Mr. Ryder. Please take
that chair by the fire. I'll just put on my slippers. . . .
Now! You want to know what happened to your
goose?"

"Oh yes, sir!"

"It came here. And quite a goose it was, too. **I don't
wonder** that you want to know about it. It laid an egg,
after it was dead. The brightest little blue egg that ever
was seen. I have it here."

Holmes opened his safe. He held up the blue
carbuncle. It shone out like a star. Ryder stared. He did
not move.

"**The game's up**, Ryder," said Holmes quietly.

At that, Ryder started to faint. "Help him to his
chair, Watson!" cried Holmes. "Give him a dash of
brandy! There. He's starting to **come to**."

The brandy brought some color back to the man's

....................................................................................

**Not one word had been said** No one talked
**I don't wonder** I am not surprised
**The game's up** We know you stole the jewel
**come to** wake up

face. "I know almost everything," said Holmes.

"Your plan was **pretty low**, wasn't it? You knew Horner had once served time in jail. So you knew the police would **pick him up** first. So what did you do? You made up some small job in the countess's room. Then you sent Horner in to do it. When Horner was done, you took the jewel. Then you called the police. Then you—"

Ryder threw himself on the rug. "Don't **turn me in**!" he begged. "I have never done wrong before."

"Get back into your chair!" said Holmes. "It's all very well for you to be sorry now. But you thought nothing of sending Mr. Horner to prison."

"I'll leave England, Mr. Holmes."

"**Hum!** We will talk about that," Holmes said. "But now let's have it. How did the stone get into the goose? How did the goose get sold? Tell us the truth, man. It's your only hope."

Ryder licked his lips. "I will tell you how it happened," said he. "The police arrested Horner. But I knew I must get the stone away at once. At any time the police might search me. There was no safe place

........................................................................................

**pretty low** very shameful

**pick him up** take him to jail; arrest him

**turn me in** tell the police

**Hum!** Really!

in the hotel.

"So I made for my sister's place. She is married to a man named Oakshott. She raises geese for market.

"All the way to my sister's, I thought every man I met was a policeman. It was a cold night. But sweat was running down my face. My sister said I looked sick. I took my pipe and went out into the yard. I wondered what would be best to do.

"I made up my mind to go to Kilburn. I knew a man there. Name of Maudsley. **He went to the bad and has just served time.** I knew Maudsley could help me sell the jewel.

"But how could I be safe? The police might stop me at any moment. They would find the stone on me. I stood looking down at the geese. Then the idea came to me.

"My sister had promised me **the pick of her geese** for my Christmas present. I would have my goose now. And that's how I would carry the stone to Kilburn!

"I caught one of the geese. It was a fine big white one, with a bar on its tail. I took it to the back of the yard. I opened its beak. The bird put up a fight. But I

........................................................................................

**He went to the bad and has just served time.** He became a criminal and has just spent time in jail.

**the pick of her geese** her best goose; any goose I wanted

**got the stone into it**.

"Just then the goose jumped from my arms. It ran back to the others. And I had to catch it again.

"I walked all the way to Kilburn with the goose. My **pal** laughed until he choked at what I had done. Then we cut open the goose. **My heart turned to water.** There was no sign of the stone! I knew there had been some terrible mistake.

"I ran back to my sister's. There was not a goose in sight! My sister had taken them all to market. She had sold them to Breckinridge."

" 'Was there another goose like the one I killed?' I asked her.

" 'Oh, yes,' she replied. 'There were two geese with bars on their tails. I never could tell them apart.'

"Well—you know the rest."

Ryder suddenly began to cry.

There was a long silence. It was broken only by the sound of Holmes's fingers, tapping. Then my friend got up. He threw open the door.

"Get out!" said he.

"What, sir? Oh, **bless you**!"

......................................................................

**got the stone into it** made it swallow the stone
**pal** friend
**My heart turned to water.** I was shocked.
**bless you** thank you

"No more words. Get out!"

And no more words were needed. There was a crash on the stairs. Then a door banged. Then we heard footsteps running away.

Holmes reached for his pipe. "I look at it this way, Watson," he said. "The police do not pay me to do their work. The countess will have her toy. The case against Horner can go nowhere unless Ryder **speaks against him**.

"That man will not **go wrong** again. He is too afraid. Send him to jail now and you make him a **jailbird for life**. Besides, it is the season to forgive.

"Now I think it's time we **looked into another bird**. Let's hope our dinner won't start us on another wild-goose chase."

---

**speaks against him** says that Horner stole the jewel

**go wrong** steal

**jailbird for life** criminal for the rest of his life

**looked into another bird** had dinner

**BEFORE YOU MOVE ON...**

1. **Sequence** What events lead to the jewel getting inside a goose?

2. **Character's Motive** Reread page 65. Why does Sherlock Holmes let Ryder get away with his crime?